For Jacquie R.

JANETTA OTTER-BARRY BOOKS

LITTLE BO PEEP copyright © Frances Lincoln Limited 2011
Text and illustrations copyright © Priscilla Lamont 2011

First published in Great Britain in 2011 and in the USA in 2012 by
Frances Lincoln Children's Books, 4 Torriano Mews,
Torriano Avenue, London NW5 2RZ
www.franceslincoln.com

A catalogue record for this book is available from the British Library

ISBN 978-1-84780-154-8

Illustrated with pen and watercolour
Set in Chalkboard

Printed in Heshan, Guangdong, China by Leo Paper Products Ltd. in March 2011

1 3 5 7 9 8 6 4 2

Nursery Rhyme Crimes

Little Bo Peep

by the sheep
as told to
PRISCILLA LAMONT

F

FRANCES LINCOLN
CHILDREN'S BOOKS

Little Bo Peep has lost her sheep
and doesn't know where to find them.
Leave them alone and they'll come home,
bringing their tails behind them.

"I'm bored!" cried Little Bo Peep that day.
"Play hide-and-seek with me."
We should have known it would end in tears –
sheep don't do games, you see.

She told us to hide while she counted to ten.
She said, "It'll all be such fun."

We tried our very best to hide

but she found us before we'd begun.

Then it was our turn to count up to ten,
which none of us knew how to do.

So we followed her round wherever she went,
while she moaned, "You haven't a clue!"

We practised for hours until in the end we'd hidden ourselves quite away.

We watched as the farmer, his son and his wife were invited to join in the fun.

A policeman turned up in the end, but still
no sheep were found, not a one!

When we came out from where we were hid,
how surprised they all were, to be sure.

But it seems that Bo Peep was sent home in disgrace –
you would think that she'd broken the law!

We know she wasn't too good at her job,
but we think it's rather a shame.
We were all having such fun on the hill
while Little Bo Peep got the blame.